I0596317

# Acknowledgements

"Sun Goddess," "Overwhelmed" and "Being Poetic" were published in La Noria 2013. "To Poe" was published in *Along the River III* 2014. "Her Eyes" was published in *Dreaming Dreams no Mortal Ever Dared to Dream Before* 2016. "Sugar Skulls" and "From the Canal" were published in *The Chachalaca Review* 2017. "White Silence" and "The Match" were published in *Credo Espoir* 2018. "Violet is" was published in *Peach Velvet* 2019.

# Table of Contents

# Yellow Eye Tea

## Diana Elizondo

FLOWERSONG
PRESS

FlowerSong Press
McAllen, Texas 78501
Copyright © 2020 by Diana Elizondo

ISBN 978-1-7345617-8-4:

Published by FlowerSong Press
in the United States of America.
www.flowersongpress.com

Set in Adobe Garamond Pro


Typeset and design by Matthew Revert
www.matthewrevert.com

## Fatigue and Broken Sanity

## Heartless Lawlessness

## Barely Clothed in Leaves

# Rose Scented Lies

# Her Eyes

Her eyes are bright yellow.
They burn through dark
corners of ceilings and walls,
watching me when I sleep or lament.
Her eyes now belong to an entity
that won't let me have seclusion
or even a sense of loneliness,
as it continues to gaze at me.
Every time I see her eyes
I'm reminded that the specter
won't let me forget how she looked
before she became the eyes in the corner.
Her once almond eyes and gentle smile
linger in my dream-like memories
while she festers in shadows
and her eyes forever glare.

# Present

Fully covered by
the snowflakes,
I wait for you to
see your gift,
I finally found
what you wanted.
Your smile is all I want
in exchange
after years of
failed attempts
and bruises
that reflect censures.
You're never satisfied
with anything I offer
nor grateful for my efforts
 result in agony.
This is my last chance
to prove my love.
Pair of ribbons shining
red across the snow
and some scissors
in my hand to perfect it.
I hope you like
your present
this time.

# Sick of Love

I'm diagnosed with a cruel ailment,
as the moths devour my insides,
sweet voices shred my mind into bits
and fire grows from endless neglect.

This sickness can't be measured
when my dignity went below zero.
The voices whisper absurd orders to
rave and kill for these sensations.

Agony breeds from every glance she gives,
she is the cause of my rose-tinted madness.

# Sea Foam

She watches creatures swimming below while floating across the sea above. At times, she peeks over shores for the couple on their morning strolls, hands entwined with affection. Though she swore to watch him, protector of sort, she still sensed no appreciation for sparing him. "He never asked where I'd gone nor spoke of me since." First, she regrets letting her have him instead of reclaiming her life back. Then she envies her fortune and finally feels hatred for his cruel apathy. Even in death, she's overwhelmed by pain from witnessing acts of passions on smooth sands.

One chilling morning, her former beloved arrives again not with his wife, but bitterness for company. In whispered curses, he stated his wife's betrayal and abandonment, a familiar site indeed. Face soaked in anger and tears he jumps into her embrace, desperate for relief. She rejects his request, letting him drown in aching misery. She would gladly pray on his behalf to at least show neutral respect, but she foolishly sold her voice years ago.

# Nightly Lover

The fangs break the skin
and soothed with a kiss.
The mysterious lover's grin
Along with a greeting hiss.
A bold angel or a kind demon,
I can't tell which it is.
All over the bare skin
the nails and fingers caress
as the sensual voice
whispers sweetness
mixed with sour lust.
The night ends in embrace
and dawn brings loneliness.
Reality's now readjust.

# I Don't Write Romance

I don't write romance
with trivial scriptures
and ailing sweetness,
no room for silk sheets
and rose scented lies,
in mindfulness.
Writing cute nothings
for hungry maidens
doesn't bring triumphs
for my existence.
I gain nothing from
exalting shallow distress
and giving false hopes
to make them frail
for beasts in crowns.

# Love Letter

Dear Beloved,

I was enchanted since the first glimpse of your glittering eyes and glossed lips. Countless years I spent in loneliness until finding you and knew we're destined to be whole. Waxed together and tied in a deep red thread so our love burns brightly in this dark world. I'll wait for the right moment for us to finally unite without disruptions with only moonlight to lighten our presence.

Becoming one by embracing you into me with force while I admire your skin, a blank canvas ready for painting. Until then, the hours are counted to the fateful night while I gaze on your beauty in a hundred photos by candlelight. No one is comparable or superior for replacement. Only you can satisfy my wants and obsessions.

Holding your neck with sharp kisses, caressing your lips and painting them in blood. Please have patience before I reward you by taking you away and bound us both in paradise, underneath the mortal feet in eternal seclusion.

p.s. See you soon.

# Sun Goddess

Light flows through the crack
barely lightens my sanctuary,
but the slit is enough to see
and I finally see the sun.

Black pearls shimmer at every glance,
her rays glisten whenever I peek
and I smile back at her gaze.

I wait for the light's return
to see her black pearls and rays
and be cleansed by contact,
yet it's not enough for me.

I want to freely worship her,
escape the solitude of darkness
and pledge myself to that goddess.

Strongly yearning to reveal my confessions,
I wished to be embraced by her,
but boldness will only leave me burned.
Fear keeps me in the shadows
and from being reduced to ash.
The sun will never know my gratitude,
but I'll always worship the goddess.

Alone and behind the door,
Peeking through the crack.

# Never Mine

Your salty lips
will never be mine.
Your small hand
I will never hold.
My affections will never
whisper into your ear.
How your heartbeat feels
I will never know.
My fingers will never
trail down your back.
You will witness
and deny my thirst.
I accept this reality,
you are never mine.

# The Match

Light up the match,
watch the flame dance,
enjoy the small warmth
and admire its grace.

Look behind the flame
he struggles and moans,
decorated in bruises
he earned from battle.

He screams muffled pleas
promising he'll be good
and show more love,
but he said that before.

Toss the match at him,
watch more flames dance,
enjoy the growing warmth
and admire true beauty.

# Werewolves and Vampires

Perfect glances and smiles
that lure lustful prey
while muscles and snarls
mix fear and awe into
dubious excitement.

Fangs succeed in piercing
the veins by whispering
sweet, empty flattery
behind reddening ears.

A beast on its hind legs
as it pants and grins
at the small creature
and pounces right in
to swallow it raw.

They all sound tempting
but their nature was never
to fulfill odd fantasies,
there's no pleasure to gain
once their teeth sink
into your bones and flesh.

Do not let silly novels
and lewd daydreams

paint your judgement
in many shades of pink,
monsters have no hearts
to give but can rip
yours away.

# Limbo is a Dream

# Dreams in Blue

Clouds covered the night sky
and streetlights stained the darkness
when I tried to find blue roses
in my search for the perfect rest.

The air was thick with lavender
and burnt blood as I strolled
under the bridge and through the cold.

I looked over my shoulder to see
floating shadows with shining eyes
going past me and down the roads
as I spat my own teeth at them.

I found a garden of red and gold roses
but the blue ones are missing.
I laid down and closed my eyes
but couldn't sleep because I failed
to find that blue rose.

# Hung

A large tree dressed in Christmas mockery
every branch wears a ring of rope
attached with dangling flesh.
The tree's accessorized in their sin.

Green leaves replaced by gray bodies
blackish wood coated with dry red,
showing evidence of assisted suicide.

All mouths open and eyes rolled up
lasting expressions before self-execution
pleading He will keep them above
unaware they're rejected long ago.

Criminals escaped punishment
Hopeless lovers chose death over loneliness,
So many reasons for self-damnation.

Unsettled by corpses hanging over my head
I lack courage to free them from their disgrace,
offering burials won't bring them redemption,
instead leave the dead displayed to warn others.

Memories haunted by morbid ornaments,
reminders that pain exists both in life and death.

# From the Bones

Predicted model of the soul,
past lives sculpted in each piece,
clues set on the beginning and end.
Words imprinted within old marrow.

Dead stripped of veins and flesh
Forcing confrontation of mortality
Reminder hidden beneath tombstones.

Snapped in half and sharpened to picks
Hunting small beasts to pierce their throats.
Skewered into rival spine or heart
Bodies contained the first weapon built.

Remains tossed across the dirt,
invented by ancient prophets in pelts.
Revealing doomsday through self-destruction.

Death silently leaves trails for living eyes,
reading worn texts from shallow graves
and telling abstract tales of ill fates.

# Blood Velvet

I'm lying on blood velvet sheets,
and inhaling another cigarette
as I stare at the cobwebs
hanging on the corners
of my beige ceiling.
Smoke dances in the air
and inside my lungs.

The need for triumphs
slowly withers as I
continue staring up
and smoking, covered
in opened letters
of disappointments.
Hardships gone in vain.

Pens abandoned
as I smoke and stare
on blood velvet sheets.

# Through the Forest

I'm lost in a forest of aging branches,
gray leaves spread throughout the ground
that looked like it's made from ashes.

Desperate to break through wooden bound
I ran down the path and found mud-
covered toads and crows piled in a mound,

On top of the carcasses and the mud,
stood a black dog with red eyes
and fangs that dripped blood.

I escaped and found a lake filled with cries
of white faces pleading me to join them.
I rowed across the lake, ignoring their cries.

On the other side I saw plastic legs in flame,
large trees with broken souls hung by death,
and crosses lying at my feet showing shame.

I stood before a chapel that lost its breath,
inside, a feral cat painted yellow, red and black
with screaming rats in its mouth.

I left the chapel through the back,
and dawn greeted at the clearing
with a mesquite tree standing.

# Sometimes I Dream

Sometimes I dream about poisoning coffees with bloody plagues and watch my enemies swallow them whole, leading armies that can break through walls with their own hands, using my hatred to turn the air into thick oil that drowns lungs, spreading just punishment to those who suppress outcasts, flying across gray skies and shoot lightning to more deserving targets, scolding the devil on his tiring antics as possessions and soul buying have become too pretentious, ripping the thorns from my skin and tossing them into hell's fire, and having a heart relieved from yearning for bitter vengeance and inflicting torment. But that only happens on rare nights.

# Smoking Room

I watch the smoke flow
out of the small cinders
like a disposed soul.
As the gray withers
and fill my skull,
the smell of ash lingers
and my mind whispers
Where do I want to go?
I look at the window
and said I don't know
as I rapidly tap my fingers.
After the smokers let out a blow
they make more gray figures
to dance to the radio
while I watch the show.

# Daring Fantasies

Tasting ink and charcoal,
painting lips and teeth,
while bringing life
into words and curses.

Thoughts of relieving urges
to break walls with godly rage,
ripping enemies' flesh from bone
and feed them to their hungry dogs.

Oh, how good would it feel to
devour ugly souls and wash
it down with tart wine
poured from black veins.

Showing hatred and spite
while breaking up their ribs,
gleefully squeezing their hearts
and draining their pride dry.

But these thoughts are just
Simply dark dreams,
necessary sins that keep
hands from turning red.

# A Dream Between

Limbo is a dream between soaring and burning where darkness and light are fused into gray plains and skies. A realm where blue opals rain from clouds as they're being exiled from above and your mouth is always savoring roses and chocolate. A region where you can gaze straight at silver eclipses without losing your eyes or run across a cactus field without being devoured by countless little fangs. A state where you decide whether you deserve to thrive in sunny valleys or wallow in dark bayous after leaving everything behind without Him lifting a finger.

# Drink Tea from a Skull

# Endless Disdain

The world wants to kill me
because my hatred towards it
brings nightmares, leaving it restless.
The world causes my teeth to turn
into powder in my mouth
and hire spider assassins
to inject brown venom into me.
In return, I fantasize how I want
the world to end, hoping for frozen
waters to drown empires or
vengeful gods to tear lands apart.
My rage blackens as strands
of my hair become thick worms
and my nights turn humid.
The cycle of anger and horror
continues until we're both laying,
gray, dry and drained.

# The Child

The child stands and stares at his porch every day when the sun is completely set. The child stands on his thin legs, staring with his sunken eyes. Frail and pale, the child stands and stares as people pass by his worn down, wooden house and yard full of weeds and long grass. The child stands without strain, staring at worn down wooden houses. He stands and stares, waiting for no one to come home. If you look close enough, you can see the child's heart through his ribs as he stands and stares.

# Little Terrorist

I caught you lurking by my window, wasting time sitting on the edge, but I saw the plan hiding in your little eyes. You were offered scraps, and praises, but your life held no value whenever you run across merciless roads. An inferior specimen both adored and loathed by everyone who's ignorant of your vendetta. One day you will lead your kind to a conquest over the giants oblivious by the tossed nuts aimed at their heads.

Your people were seen spreading plague and stealing power, yet you were never prosecuted due to your docile persona, your tail waving behind your back and a delicate face that lies. Your swift reflexes and shyness hides a plotter of human genocide from the pines, spying and calculating.

# Moments of Horror

Don't look out the windows,
la lechuza is watching.
Stay inside the house,
la chupacabra is hunting.
Get away from the river,
la llorona is walking there.


Try staying awake,
Freddy's coming for you.
Don't go camping,
Jason will chop you in two.
Don't watch the tape,
you'll die in seven days.


Warn your child to behave,
o las brujas will eat them.
Check under the bed,
el cucuy might be there.
Follow the rules,
Ghost face is on the prowl.


Take caution on Hallows Eve,
the boogeyman's coming home.

Listen to the nightly wind,
the children are singing tonight.
You don't have to go outside,
it's natural to be afraid of the dark.

# Nevermore

I only feel rain as I lie on the concrete and filth,
waiting for my soul to drift and my body to stiffen.
Reliving the heartaches and self-destruction in my mind
brings me encouragement to stay on the ground,
I'm tired of thinking of the reasons to struggle anymore,
besides feeding my torment and despair to my muse.
Ravens, black cats and madness brought fame
as they thrived from years of sorrow and agony.
My craft had to spawn from a price I had to pay.
Throughout my journey of searching for achievement and love,
I've been abandoned and neglected many times
by those who claimed to love me then leave, and others
who hated me because they see no worth in my existence.
The bars were the only sanctums I can escape for a while,
but they can't ease the pain that life kept inflicting on me.
Endless gray and showers bring me some comfort,
knowing that I shall suffer nevermore.

# The New Witch

The witch drinks tea from a skull
and smokes lavender with her pipe
ignoring God and Satan's squabble.
The witch rather focuses on feeding
on Earth's bounties for power
by draining rivers dry
and stripping trees of their fruit
than find someone to share with.
The witch lives in isolation, not loneliness
as she leaves rejected suitors behind
with blades pierced into their loins.
The witch inhales burning blood
and bathes in violet fumes
when she performs rituals and chants
to enhance her talents in her artwork,
while setting her enemies on fire
and reducing their souls to cinder.
She's not good or wicked,
she's simply a new kind of witch.

# To Poe

Hope the abyss was kind to bring eternal rest
from vulgar sadness, unachieved hopes and maddening fears
freed from the progress of physical and mental disease.

May Death reunite lost loves in permanent embrace
know your dark muse had succeeded her purpose
years of bleeding ink and spilling torment not in vain.

Happiness absent in tales of death and woe
haunting minds with vengeful cats and hideous hearts.
Ominous ravens forever imprinted in history.

Dedications through black plums and blood petals.
Written hardships will never be forgotten.

# Omens

In the news,
crowds marching,
foaming with
frustration
and loathing
as volcanos
spit fiery blood
and storms
scream flood.

# Spiral

My brain tries to crawl out,
cracking the skull open from inside.
My veins tearing apart by crazed thoughts
flashing behind closed eyes as whispers,
cackles and shattering glass
echo in my ears every night.

My heart pounds against my ribs
to get more blood to end its thirst,
but the want for relief is never fulfilled.
I'm holding on what's left of my mind
while betrayed by both dark and light.

The pain in my lungs are drowning me
as fear of monsters and damnation keep
pushing me through the mattress and
floor as I spiral further into the abyss.

# Fatigue and Broken Sanity

# I had to be

I had to be very bored to find the ring inside my mug more amusing than doing anything else. I finished my coffee, but I still sat by my table, staring at the brown ring inside the mug. I wanted to take a bath, but I stayed on my chair, staring inside my mug. I thought about getting dressed and driving my way to work, instead I took a closer look in my mug hoping to find more excuses to stay. I grabbed the mug's handle, but let my fingers slip from it like I did with everything else. I thought maybe I could sit here until the brown ring permanently stains the mug and see if it can get anymore filthy, or I could sit here until I become a brittle corpse with dry skin still tight around my bones. I had to be desperate or depressed to let a mug keep me on my chair.

# Being Poetic

Beauty spawned from destructions,
displayed in sheets scarred by ink
and infliction exposes raw emotions.
Sublime passions and nightmarish links
force minds to spill hallucinations.

Mental masochism and great straining
as thoughts boil inside a globe of bone
manifesting into a vicious offspring
breaking through membranes like stone.

Seeking old idols to replace a muse
from scriptures and scented smoke.
In a nocturnal trance, words ooze
through pens with every stroke.

Gaining loved ones and casting hexes,
summoning Wrath to spit acid at society,
expressing personal ideals and new senses
from great fatigue and broken sanity.

# Word-craft

Lighting the candles
and summoning spirits
cloaked in violet and red
while pulling out my cauldron
and chant new spells again.
one line after the other,
but they bring nothing,
so I shook the smoke away
and try another chant.
The spirits dance around
the candle's flame
as I say the new lines
with growing volume
and I know that I
have a new spell at last.
Until the reds and violets
fade, abandoning the flame
and leaving me disappointed.
I put out the candle and
the cauldron away as I
wallow in my bed once again.

# Violent Specter

House plagued by spectral burden,
once flesh now malevolent parasite
rose out of the dirt after the mind deceased.

No exorcism can appease the accursed presence
nor the rabid spirit can be restrained
from slamming doors and breaking through walls.

Banshee cries and shattered glasses heard in halls
countless nights without blissful silence
no dreams for struggling sleepers.

Long since it lost all senses
remorse, sympathy and humanity
gone from lethal consumption for escapism.
Apathetic towards loss of reality
blindly roaming across floors without shame
forcefully sharing its misery to living kin.
Born with high expectations, but never achieved.
Now dead and haunting a broken home.

# Playing Nocturnal

The night's hanging on edge
as darkness barely holds its ground
and silence still creeping in the halls.
Still awake, I listen to plucked strings
that remind the past years of gold,

All alone and undisturbed,
I watch my room grow dim
and my pages turn from bare
to stained in written nonsense.
Inspiration never comes at 4:30 a.m.

After spending the last hours
playing a tortured, nocturnal writer,
the bewitching sensation fades
as dawn arrives to devour the night.

# Ridding the Block

Trapped in a bright screen of white nothingness, my fingers are glued to the black keys and irritating me like an incurable itch. No words to say or think, wasted hours in suspended stillness, hoping for the test of patience to end. I frowned at the realization of this conflict, my muse has abandoned me. I left my position to begin the quest to find inspiration.

Filling my room with burned vampire blood to absorb the scent and refresh my mind, but no motivation came from incense intoxication. I pondered while sipping coffee and sitting on black tiles, glaring at the white walls that mocked at my unfortunate state. The ridicule brought more strength for the frustration to break through the borders of my mentality. Madness had been accepted and embraced; I rammed into the wall.

Repeatedly bashing my head against the cruel mocker with maniacal force as I finally marked on the insulting wall. Bizarre sensation overcame me, words formed inside and I smiled at my success as inspiration flowed through. My fingers reached for the keys, but the screen went black as weakening eyes stared back at me. The crimson flow bled dry.

# White Silence

Silence flows through,
into my room
without introduction.
Silence hovers over me,
keeping me from knowing
what I need to do with my time.
Silence spreads white veils,
covering and fading the colors
from all over my room.
Silence lingers and annoys
as I grow bored from waiting.
Silence suggests I try lamenting
and let my thoughts spill out.
Silence whispers they're all true,
causing me to curl up in my bed.
Tears fall from my eyes quietly,
as Silence keeps me company.

# I have Nothing

I have nothing to give
and nothing to say
when I know nothing.

I lived for 35 years
and still know nothing
how existence works.

The world is brutal
but I don't know why
or how I'm still alive.

We're all going to die
but I don't know when
or if we'll face it together.

I have nothing to say,
I have nothing to give.
I still know nothing.

# Dreaming Insomnia

The taste of blood lingers all night after ripping the serpent's stomach to free the tiger inside. My jaws are aching and breaking from losing my wisdom teeth to scales and flesh. The agony robs me from sleep and enslaves me to wonder how the world's decline is taking toll, forgiveness is pointless and hating doesn't make progress. From dreamless slumbers to episodes of sleepless dreams, I sometimes question if I want to live any longer as I lay abandoned in my bed without rest.

I stare at the black sky through the window curtains and the ceiling through the darkness as the need for small deaths can't be satisfied. Annoyed by the on and off relationship with the night, I learned that numbness is the only way to end the subtle torment, but the prayers are never answered, and I continue faking dreams while lying awake.

# Process

Locked away from distractions,
voices, contacts and conflicts
to keep me from losing my pen.
Sealed away in coldness,
isolation, walls and muse calls
to keep me from leaving.
Deeply influenced by smokes,
nightmares, and lavender
to keep my fingers bent.
Possessed by songs, rage,
Tragedies and despair
To keep my mind flowing.
I must thrive in thinking,
Writing, stretching and reading
To keep me from dying.

# Heartless Lawlessness

# Sugar Skulls

Sugar skulls are placed by tombstones,
along with bouquets and photos.
They can also be found by the river
And sometimes floating in it.
Sugar skulls are seen being tossed
over walls, in the canals or even hung on
thin branches of mesquite trees.
These sweet offerings are found
in several places so the departed
can know they're not forgotten.

# Dead Sheep

The shepherd drags
dozens of dead sheep,
ropes around their necks.

Some mauled by wolves,
others have skulls split
to silence their screams,
and few starved to death.

Carcasses grow heavier
and flesh keeps rotting,
the shepherd keeps dragging.

# I am Nightmare

I stalk you in the alleys
with carnal urges in mind
and a knife in hand.
I turn you into stone
and break your manhood
with my venomous glare.
I offer your children candy
and rip out their limbs
once your back is turned.
I stand in your way
wearing blood black skin
that brings you hate and dread.
I scream justice in your ear
while you sleep in your silk sheets,
inside your luxurious fortress.
I'm the rebel with horns
that challenges the scriptures
your ego desperately thrives.
I'm everything everyone fears.

# Effortless

Hungry,
angry
for and of
bloodshed
spawned from
heartless
lawlessness
within fluoride
fueled
inner
genocide
ordered by
flat screen heads
filling people's dreads.
I've tried,
but
I'm tired
making threats
and wishing deaths.
I'm done
and now gone.

# Overwhelmed

Humanity spiraling beyond devolution
revolting wild beasts with outrageous acts
fueled by sadism, instead of ancestral instinct.
Disappointments committed in gleeful ignorance.

Hopelessly searching an ounce of improvement,
observations taking toll, tired of atrocious reruns
performed by various eras, none learned a damn thing.

Civilizations prevent progress with countless dead-ends,
harsh labyrinths, built miles wide without exits
mocking poor fools wanting equal happiness
such privileges reserved for promoters of hate.

From furs to suits, instincts reduced to civilized savagery
playing Death excused for symptoms of mental disease
with possessive paranoia or offerings to Lovecraftian gods.

Life and media blended from poorly structured barriers
bringing confusion in knowing reality,
lunatics exploited by screens, despised in awe.
Gaining credit from both infamy and praise.

Species' progression fueled by deadly sins
apathy is the key to human existence.
Like wire, denial suffocates and tightens.

# I Tried to Die

I wake up with fragmented memories
of witnessing heaven and hell.
from glimpses of crystal cities
to blood filled seashores,
I gain little satisfaction of clips
about being in the afterlife.
They keep draining from my ears
like wine leaking through cracks
as I forget what I saw every night.
I'm tired of dragging myself around
after dying and coming back many times
with a sore spine and numb jaws.
when will these slumbers lead me
to my true escape from here
and achieve actual rest?

I admit redemption's far from arrival.
The messenger enters, his smile fades
looking down at my new third eye.
Heated barrel in one hand,
crumbled paper in another.

Just another overwhelmed fool
forget the note and take me away.

# Someday

Someday you'll learn true hatred is spawned from hearing the bile pouring out of your mouth, spreading pain and ignorance at every breath.

Someday you'll realize how wrong you are as I punctured the truth through your skull leaving you speechless and dumb.

Someday you'll wish you never been born in grand social privilege, exempted from the repression inflicted by holy-scriptures and phallic ideals.

Someday you'll know what unfairness is when you see the sharp blades in my eyes wielded by years of disdain towards your pathetic existence.

Someday you'll know regret when I cross your path ripping each muscle tissue from your bones while you scream unanswered prayers.

Someday you'll feel despair like your victims had when you brought misery and repression birthed by your arrogance. Hopeless and abandoned.

Someday you'll suffer great guilt and self-loathing, knowing that you motivated me to forever hunt for your hollow head.

Someday I'll learn to dismiss your morals and bravely show you how much I wished for your fall to be ungraceful.

Someday I'll succeed in becoming the monster you think I am as I consume your world with fiery fangs.

Someday I'll find a way to rid the bane of everyone's existence without being judged for being the beast I became.

Someday you'll recognize the ugly monstrosity you created.

# From My Tower

From my tower,
I see the entire race going mad
and using their knowledge to waste everything.
From my tower,
I see them descending into denial
as they kill and poison for faith and profit.
From my tower,
I see their evolution spiraling to disorder
when humanity is replaced with animal urges.
From my tower,
I see ancient sinners being reborn
with every atrocity repeated through time.
From my tower,
I see children abandoning innocence too young
as they burn, fire and slay out of boredom.
From my tower,
I see frost spreading like a biblical disease
while humans refuse to take responsibility.
From my tower,
I see Cthulhu slowly claiming the continents
as icebergs melt and waters rise.
From my tower,
I see no hope for redemption

# The Mosque

The mosque stood pure
in a friendly looking town.
The mosque stood pure
as prayers are said to God.
The mosque stood pure
and untouched by malice.
The mosque stood pure
until the men came one night
and forced themselves inside.
They ripped, tore, spilled blood
and left the mosque in her shame.
The mosque stood broken
as the people cried and asked why,
but are ignored by the ones
who only protect God's true home.
The people fixed and rebuilt the wooden
frames and removed the blood.
The mosque looked pure,
But the fear still lingered inside
as prayers are said to God.

# From the Canal

A corpse is found. The veins visible on gray skin coated in grass stains and mud. The arms are bent backwards, and elbows broken from impact. Blonde hair is now dyed in greenish brown and nails cracked to the tips. The corpse is missing a pink slipper and a shirt, exposing a full belly. The eyes, wide and faded, look up from the bottom of the canal. "Is it an accident or a new addition tossed into the collection?" asked the officers staring back down at her wide faded eyes.

# Barely Clothed in Leaves

# In the Rain

I sit in the rain
hoping it will
drown me with
its heavy showers.
The rain soaks
my skin as they leak
through until they reach
right to my bones.
The wet and cold
become unpleasant,
but I'm still breathing.
I inhale deeply
to get the drops fill
up my throat and lungs.
I'm still breathing
in the wet and the cold
as I sit in the rain.

# All's the Same

Strands of ebony
become strings of pearl
but all's the same.
Memories fade
as tragedies increase
but all's the same.
Skin gains blotches
and loses smoothness
but all's the same.
Hopes are delusions,
so are goals now
but all's the same.
People change
and later buried
but all's the same.

# The Moth

The moth fluttered attempting to break through the window. Gray, thin wings tapping against the glass, but can't make an inch-long scratch. Flying high and low, the moth kept searching for a way out. I pushed her off the window to a new route. The moth denied my aid and stayed in her self-made prison. Rejected, I left the moth to proceed with her pointless efforts. Hoping she'll be gone when I return.

I returned and greeted again by wings fluttering to nowhere. I gently trapped the moth in my hands, freeing her from the invisible wall, holding her in a warm cup. The moth calmly sat as I showed her the door and opened my hands. Still perched on my fingers, the moth offered me her trust. I repaid her by exhaling a strong blow, sending her back to the sky.

# Displays of Eden

Decorated with white and violet blooms, the front yard's ground coated in lush greens and palms reached heavenly height. Birds, cats and even possums visit the site, remembering the divine days of paradise before His latest creation.

Through the kitchen window exhibits a garden hose coiled around a lemon tree. The dusty, worn snake rests from committing temptation, stripping Man further of innocence. The fallen fruit rotting beneath the shade leaving original sin's still lingering, sour scent.

The backyard filled with dry patches, no bright flowers except grass losing tone. A tree, its only inhabitant and barely clothed in leaves, reenacts the moral destruction caused by filthy disobedience. Earth forever tainted by divine loss, but mostly by dogs.

# Resolutions

Things change yearly at midnight
people with memory loss would say,
unaware that the world goes around
one way and never the other.

Changes are asked and promised
but left forgotten in dusty shields
to be buried with others before them.

Their lives continue after those nights
despite overwhelming fruitlessness.
Nothing good ever happens at midnight.

# Winter Valley

Sense of loneliness
arrives in gray skies
and coldness,
leading self-entrapment
within cities and suburbs.
The bold few wander
through cruel conditions
of that isolation
where missing snow is
common in southern borders.
All forced to wallow alone
in the gray chills,
avoiding contact
to distract themselves
from the festering cold,
unaware of what they lost.

# We Wait

A waiting game
we're forced to play.
Since first breath
we do things
to pass time.
Few achieved a lot,
others did little
or none.
Some longer,
others sooner.
The game can end
when He says it,
someone else,
or we see fit.
Birth to death
is not living,
but waiting.
We're waiting.

# Unwanted Visitor

You're not invited when you
distract victims from the journeys
in the comfortable, velvet sheets.

Growing tired of your whispers
slithering in their ears to burrow
into the shadows of their skulls.

Your presence is not worth enduring
when it brings live nightmares,
driving people to think endlessly.

They lose interest in the sightings
and experiences outside visible plains.
You always bring aching delusions.

You should be thrown out the window,
shards raining over your remains.
Your death will cure their ailments.

Freeing sleepers to see the world warp
from ancient cities to glass oceans.
Freed from your unwanted visits.

# The House with the Red Door

There's a gray house in my neighborhood where I used to walk by every morning. Light gray bricks, dark gray roof, everything is gray except for the front door. A small wooden door that's red like cheap lipstick. The house with the red door became stranger as I wondered what kind of chaos lurked inside. A boy picking his skin with a knife? A frail man yelling at his mannequin wife? A teenage girl plotting mass murder? A cold room where someone committed suicide? A door that red must lock wicked things away from anyone to see. I stopped walking by the gray house, but its red door is still imprinted in my memory.

# One More Time

"You can't keep me out,"
he yells at the front door.
He again begs to be let in.
Mom can't leave him
in this nowhere town,
alone and penniless.
He knocks harder
cracking the door's
glass like last time.
He just wants cash
to drink one more time.
Only one bottle
for this day, "I swear,"
"I mean it this time."
He screams and pleads,
"Please, just let me in!"
Mom walks to her room,
ignoring his cries at last.

# Season to Mourn

"You can't keep me out,"
All the citrus leaves died
after falling from their branches
as the chill breeze grew stronger.

The orange grins rotted away
as ghosts returned to their graves
replaced by snowy smiles.

Pumpkins and screams
buried in frozen tears
as white sheets descend.

# Violet is

The night pushing
the sun down,
drowning it
in darkness.

A bouquet of
lavender filling
the air with
its strong perfume.

A somber song
about love lost
after ten years.

A midnight breeze
that gently cools
the weary skin.

A color of a kiss
that no one
wants to have.

Diana Elizondo was born in Laredo, Texas, but spent most of her life in McAllen Texas. Her writing inspirations are Sylvia Plath, Robert Frost and Edgar Allen Poe. She earned her Master's degree in English at University of Texas Pan American and her M.F.A degree in Creative Writing at University of Texas Rio Grande Valley. Her first book, *Smoked Blood and Lavender*, was released in 2017. Diana was also an adjunct English instructor for Texas A&M International University, Texas A&M University Kingsville and is now teaching for Texas Southmost College in Brownsville Texas.

www.ingramcontent.com/pod-product-compliance
Lightning Source LLC
Chambersburg PA
CBHW010644100726
47900CB00011B/2971